The
Keeping Quilt

Reprinted by arrangement with Simon & Schuster Books for Young Readers,
a Division of Simon & Schuster Inc., for Silver Burdett Ginn Inc.

SIMON AND SCHUSTER BOOKS FOR YOUNG READERS,
Simon & Schuster Building,
Rockefeller Center,
1230 Avenue of the Americas,
New York, New York 10020.

1 2 3 4 5 6 7 8 9 10 RRD 98 97 96 95 94 93

Library of Congress Cataloging-in-Publication Data
Polacco, Patricia. The keeping quilt. Summary: A homemade quilt ties together the
lives of four generations of an immigrant Jewish family, remaining a symbol of their
enduring love and faith.
[1. Quilts—Fiction.   2. Jews—Fiction.   3. Emigration and immigration—Fiction]   I. Title.
PZ7.P75186Ai   1988   [E]   88-4507
ISBN 0-663-56228-7

The Keeping Quilt

By Patricia Polacco

Simon and Schuster Books for Young Readers, Published by Simon & Schuster, Inc. New York

When my Great-Gramma Anna came to America,
she wore the same thick overcoat and big boots she
had worn for farm work. But her family weren't dirt
farmers anymore. In New York City her father's work
was hauling things on a wagon, and the rest of the
family made artificial flowers all day.

Everyone was in a hurry, and it was so crowded,
not like in backhome Russia. But all the same it was
their home, and most of their neighbors were just
like them.

When Anna went to school, English sounded to her like pebbles dropping into shallow water. *Shhhhhh….Shhhhhh…. Shhhhhh*. In six months she was speaking English. Her parents almost never learned, so she spoke English for them, too.

The only things she had left of backhome Russia were her
dress and the babushka she liked to throw up into the air
when she was dancing.

And her dress was getting too small. After her mother had sewn her a new one, she took her old dress and babushka. Then from a basket of old clothes she took Uncle Vladimir's shirt, Aunt Havalah's nightdress, and an apron of Aunt Natasha's.

"We will make a quilt to help us always remember home," Anna's mother said. "It will be like having the family in backhome Russia dance around us at night."

And so it was. Anna's mother invited all the neighborhood ladies. They cut out animals and flowers from the scraps of clothing. Anna kept the needles threaded and handed them to the ladies as they needed them. The border of the quilt was made of Anna's babushka.

On Friday nights Anna's mother would say the prayers that started the Sabbath. The family ate challah and chicken soup. The quilt was the tablecloth.

Anna grew up and fell in love with Great-Grandpa Sasha.
To show he wanted to be her husband, he gave
Anna a gold coin, a dried flower, and a piece of
rock salt, all tied into a linen handkerchief.
The gold was for wealth, the flower
for love, and the salt so their
lives would have flavor.
    She accepted the hankie.
They were engaged.

Under the wedding huppa, Anna and Sasha promised each other love and understanding. After the wedding, the men and women celebrated separately.

When my Grandma Carle was born, Anna wrapped her daughter in the quilt to welcome her warmly into the world. Carle was given a gift of gold, flower, salt, and bread. Gold so she would never know poverty, a flower so she would always know love, salt so her life would always have flavor, and bread so that she would never know hunger.

Carle learned to keep the Sabbath and to cook and clean and do washing.

"Married you'll be someday," Anna told Carle, and…

again the quilt became a wedding huppa, this time for Carle's wedding to Grandpa George. Men and women celebrated together, but they still did not dance together. In Carle's wedding bouquet was a gold coin, bread, and salt.

Carle and George moved to a farm in Michigan and
Great-Gramma Anna came to live with them. The quilt
once again wrapped a new little girl, Mary Ellen.

Mary Ellen called Anna, Lady Gramma. She had grown very old and was sick a lot of the time. The quilt kept her legs warm.

On Anna's ninety-eighth birthday, the cake was a kulich,
a rich cake with raisins and candied fruit in it.

When Great-Gramma Anna died, prayers were said to lift her soul to heaven. My mother Mary Ellen was now grown up.

When Mary Ellen left home, she took the quilt with her.

When she became a bride, the quilt became her huppa. For the first time, friends who were not Jews came to the wedding. My mother wore a suit, but in her bouquet were gold, bread, and salt.

The quilt welcomed me, Patricia, into the world...

and it was the tablecloth for my first birthday party.

At night I would trace my fingers around the edges of each animal on the quilt before I went to sleep. I told my mother stories about the animals on the quilt. She told me whose sleeve had made the horse, whose apron had made the chicken, whose dress had made the flowers, and whose babushka went around the edge of the quilt.

The quilt was a pretend cape when I was in the bullring,
or sometimes a tent in the steaming Amazon jungle.

At my wedding to Enzo-Mario, men and women danced together. In my bouquet were gold, bread, and salt—and a sprinkle of wine, so I would always know laughter.

Twenty years ago I held Traci Denise in the quilt for the first time. Someday she, too, will leave home and she will take the quilt with her.